MENTAL HEALTH CRISIS

Anxiety and Depression

ON THE RISE

Kristina Castillo

ReferencePoint Press

San Diego, CA

About the Author

Kristina Castillo is a writer originally from South Carolina. She writes books for children and teens.

© 2023 ReferencePoint Press, Inc.
Printed in the United States

For more information, contact:
ReferencePoint Press, Inc.
PO Box 27779
San Diego, CA 92198
www.ReferencePointPress.com

Picture Credits:
Cover: Tinnakorn jorruang/Shutterstock.com
6: Leonard Zhokovsky/Shutterstock.com
10: CHAIWATPHOTOS/Shutterstock.com
12: LightField Studios/Shutterstock.com
18: Beatriz Vera/Shutterstock.com
22: Ringo Chiu/Shutterstock.com
27: Lev radin/Shutterstock.com
31: Stephanie Kenner/Shutterstock.com
35: Maury Aaseng
39: iStock
41: SolStock/iStock
47: SeventyFour/Shutterstock.com
49: Giselleflissak/iStock
53: BearFotos/Shutterstock.com

LIBRARY OF CONGRESS CATALOGING-IN-PUBLICATION DATA

Names: Castillo, Kristina C., author.
Title: Anxiety and depression on the rise / by Kristina C. Castillo.
Description: San Diego, CA : ReferencePoint Press, 2022. | Series: Mental health crisis | Includes bibliographical references and index.
Identifiers: LCCN 2021047233 (print) | LCCN 2021047234 (ebook) | ISBN 9781678202743 (library binding) | ISBN 9781678202750 (ebook)
Subjects: LCSH: Anxiety--Juvenile literature. | Depression in adolescence--Juvenile literature.
Classification: LCC BF575.A6 C377 2022 (print) | LCC BF575.A6 (ebook) | DDC 155.4/1246--dc23
LC record available at https://lccn.loc.gov/2021047233
LC ebook record available at https://lccn.loc.gov/2021047234

CONTENTS

Spotlight on Mental Health

In May 2021 twenty-three-year-old Naomi Osaka, a professional tennis player, was scheduled to compete in the French Open. Shortly before the tournament, Osaka announced that she would not be participating in any post-match interviews due to the anxiety they caused her. "I am not a natural public speaker and get huge waves of anxiety before I speak to the world's media,"[1] said Osaka. When she did not attend the press conference following her first-round victory, Osaka was fined $15,000. She was also warned that she could be expelled from the tournament for not speaking to the press. The next day she announced that she was withdrawing from the French Open. She explained that she was taking a break from tennis because she was concerned about her mental health. In her announcement on Twitter, Osaka shared that she had experienced periods of depression and anxiety as a high-profile athlete. "The truth is that I have suffered long bouts of depression since the U.S. Open in 2018 and I have had a really hard time coping with that,"[2] she said. Osaka is an example of a very successful young person affected by anxiety and depression.

Anxiety and Depression Are Common

Like Osaka, many people who have anxiety also have depression and vice versa. Almost 50 percent of people diagnosed with depression are also diagnosed with an anxiety disorder. Anxiety and depression are the most common mental illnesses. According to the Centers for Disease Control and Prevention (CDC), in 2019, 15 percent of the US adult population reported anxiety symptoms and 18.5 percent reported depressive symptoms within the previous two weeks.

Given the prevalence of anxiety and depression, most people are affected by these disorders in some way, either personally or indirectly through a family member or close friend. In an essay Osaka penned for *Time* magazine after the French Open, she acknowledged this. "It has become apparent to me that literally everyone either suffers from issues related to their mental health or knows someone who does," she wrote. "The number of messages I received from such a vast cross section of people confirms that."[3]

The prevalence of these disorders is concerning because anxiety and depression can interfere with one's quality of life. They can affect relationships, make it difficult to socialize, and hamper one's ability to perform well at school or work. Further, untreated anxiety and depression can lead to serious health problems, such as heart problems, stroke, and even suicide. Recognizing the symptoms of anxiety and depression is important so that people can obtain professional treatment.

Surge in Anxiety and Depression

Experts have been seeing an increase in anxiety and depression in adults, teens, and children, particularly during the pandemic. Some reports indicate that the rates of anxiety and depression have doubled or tripled since the pandemic began. According to a CDC survey, almost 31 percent of Americans reported symptoms of anxiety or depression in June 2020, which was fairly early in the pandemic. As of January 2021, that number had increased

Tennis champion Naomi Osaka, of Japan, is one of several professional athletes who have recently publicly admitted to suffering from depression and anxiety.

to 41 percent. Uncertainty about the future, job loss or reduction, and COVID-19 itself all fueled mental health disorders. Former first lady Michelle Obama experienced what she termed "low-grade depression" during the pandemic. "I'm waking up in the middle of the night because I'm worrying about something or there's a heaviness,"[4] she said.

Young people are experiencing anxiety and depression at higher levels than ever. The pandemic has disrupted young people's lives and isolated them from their peers and activities. School closures have limited students' access to mental health resources and support systems. News reports have highlighted the increase in young patients in crisis in emergency departments. Jenna

Glover, the director of psychology training at Children's Hospital Colorado, says, "We really have never seen anything like this rapid growth in kids presenting with mental health problems and the severity of those problems. I've never seen this in my entire career."[5] According to experts, the pandemic has highlighted and amplified a mental health crisis in the United States and worldwide. The mental health fallout from the pandemic is predicted to last for years.

Light at the End of the Tunnel

Recently, people have become more open about mental health, and many celebrities and athletes have spoken out about their struggles. During the Summer Olympics held in Tokyo in 2021, world-class gymnast Simone Biles withdrew from several competitions to focus on her mental health. Her decision, which received a lot of support from fans and the media, reiterated the importance of mental health in addition to physical health. Like Osaka, Biles recognized when it was in her best interest not to compete. Although Osaka does not wish to be a spokesperson for mental health, she says she "hope[s] that people can relate and understand it's O.K. to not be O.K., and it's O.K. to talk about it. There are people who can help, and there is usually light at the end of any tunnel."[6]

> "It's O.K. to not be O.K., and it's O.K. to talk about it. There are people who can help, and there is usually light at the end of any tunnel."[6]
>
> —Naomi Osaka, professional tennis player

CHAPTER ONE

What Are Anxiety and Depression?

Anxiety and depression are common mental health disorders. In fact, anxiety and depression are the most prevalent mental illnesses in the United States. These disorders are potentially debilitating, and unfortunately, they appear to be more widespread today than in years past.

An estimated 40 million adults in the United States—19 percent of the population—have an anxiety disorder. In other words, nearly one in five adults in the United States has an anxiety disorder, making it the most common mental illness in the United States. Depression is the second most common mental illness. It is estimated that more than 19 million adults in the United States—nearly 8 percent of the population—have at least one major depressive episode every year.

People of all ages and all racial, ethnic, and socioeconomic backgrounds experience anxiety and depression. However, anxiety and depression affect some groups more than others. For example, women are more likely to experience anxiety and depression than are men. During 2020, the first year of the pandemic, young people were more likely to experience anxiety and depression than any other age group.

Although there is no single cause of anxiety and depression, there are known risk factors, including genetic and environmental factors. Some factors are unchangeable, but some, such as avoiding drugs and alcohol, are within one's control. Understanding these disorders and recognizing possible symptoms are critical for seeking help early.

Anxiety

Anxiety is worry or tension due to fear, and it is accompanied by physical changes like increased blood pressure. Everyone experiences anxiety and stress from time to time. For example, many people are anxious when they have to speak in public, but that anxiety can be lessened with preparation and practice. Many students are stressed before an exam, which can also be reduced by adequate preparation. In fact, anxiety is a natural reaction to a threat or stress, and it is considered a survival mechanism. In the face of danger, anxiety is responsible for triggering the body's fight-or-flight response. This response produces multiple physical changes, including increased blood flow, that assist the body in dealing with life-threatening situations, such as fighting against (fight) or running away from (flight) the threat.

However, when anxiety happens at inappropriate times, too frequently, and too intensely for too long, anxiety is considered a disorder. Recurring intrusive thoughts or worries are common with anxiety disorders. People with anxiety disorders may avoid certain situations out of fear. On most days they may feel more anxious than not. Some people with anxiety may also experience physical symptoms, such as sweating, trembling, breathing quickly, or a rapid heartbeat.

When a person experiences stress, hormones like adrenaline and cortisol flood the body. When a person is in a constant state of anxiety, these hormones are released too much, making it difficult to remain calm, even during non-stressful times. For people with anxiety, the amygdala, which serves as the brain's threat-detection system, may detect a threat even when there is none. Anxiety may also weaken the connection between the amygdala and the prefrontal cortex of the brain, which is responsible for analyzing information and making rational decisions. Thus, when an anxious person's brain receives a threat message from the amygdala, the response may be out of proportion to the threat.

Anxiety may not be visible to others. Hara Howard, a licensed professional counselor, has experienced panic attacks since childhood. Despite being, in Howard's words, "a typical child with a bubbly personality,"[7] Howard was secretly struggling with anxiety, which caused uncomfortable feelings, worried thoughts, and even shame.

There are several types of anxiety disorders, including generalized anxiety disorder, panic disorder, and specific phobic disorders. Generalized anxiety disorder is characterized by excessive nervousness and worry about multiple situations or activities. Panic disorder is a condition whereby people suffer from repeat-

Every year high school and college students suffer from anxiety. Medical professionals say that the condition is a natural reaction to stress and therefore a type of survival mechanism.

ed panic attacks. A panic attack is the sudden onset of extreme stress, anxiety, or fear. A panic attack is generally accompanied by physical and emotional symptoms, such as chest pain, dizziness, sweating, trembling, hot flashes or chills, shortness of breath, fear of dying, and feelings of detachment. People with other anxiety disorders may also experience panic attacks. Panic attacks usually last less than thirty minutes, with the most intense symptoms resolving within ten minutes of onset. Specific phobic disorders refer to an irrational fear of a specific situation or object that is persistent and intense. Examples include claustrophobia (fear of confined spaces) and arachnophobia (fear of spiders).

> "Sometimes I can co-exist peacefully with it. I am able to recognize it for what it is and move on with my day. And then, sometimes, I feel like I am completely losing control."[8]
>
> —Ashley Fisher, anxiety sufferer

Symptoms of Anxiety

Anxiety disorders are a group of related disorders. Each disorder has its own set of symptoms. However, all anxiety disorders have one thing in common: persistent and excessive fear or worry about ordinary situations. Worried thoughts or fears often run in a loop, like a song on repeat. People with anxiety disorders may experience a variety of emotional and physical symptoms. Emotional symptoms may include feeling apprehensive, being tense or jumpy, feeling restless or irritable, anticipating the worst, and being watchful for signs of danger. Physical symptoms may include a pounding or racing heart, shortness of breath, sweating, tremors, headaches, fatigue, insomnia, upset stomach, and frequent urination or diarrhea.

Ashley Fisher, who has experienced anxiety since childhood, never knows when her anxiety will arise. She explains, "Sometimes I can co-exist peacefully with it. I am able to recognize it for what it is and move on with my day. And then, sometimes, I feel like I am completely losing control."[8] She experiences physical symptoms

such as a racing heart and trembling, and has spiraling thoughts. Although some people can identify their triggers, she explains that she often does not know what triggers her anxiety.

Sometimes, anxiety appears alongside other mental health disorders like depression. In fact, anxiety can be a symptom of depression. Similarly, depression can be caused by anxiety.

Depression

Depression is more than just feeling sad or a case of the blues for a few days. Depression is a feeling of intense sadness or despair that interferes with daily living. People with depression usually lack interest in activities they previously enjoyed. Depression may be triggered by an event or may arise out of nowhere.

When someone experiences the death of a loved one, the person typically feels grief. Grief and depression are similar, but there are some differences. Grief tends to decrease over time and, after an initial grieving period, may resurface in waves, usually triggered by a memory. Depression tends to be more intense and persistent. Sometimes it is difficult to tell whether someone is experiencing grief or depression.

Some people mistakenly believe that depression is not a serious illness or is something that can be ignored. Depression is not a sign of weakness or something that a person can simply shrug off. It is also not a character flaw. Instead, it is a serious medical condition with real symptoms that can be treated.

Some people only experience one depressive episode during their lifetime. However, many people who experience depression have multiple episodes. Without treatment, episodes can last a few months to several years.

Untreated depression can change the brain. Some research has shown that parts of the brain can shrink during depressive episodes, which may impact the functioning of the shrunken parts. For example, the hippocampus, which is associated with memory and learning functions, can noticeably shrink after an eight-month depressive episode. Also, research has shown a connection between depression and inflammation in the brain, although it is unclear whether depression causes the inflammation or vice versa. Oxygen can be restricted in the body when a person is depressed, which can also impact the brain, resulting in inflammation and brain cell injury. More research is needed to determine whether depressive episodes cause long-term changes in memory, mood, or functioning.

Although common, depression is a serious mental illness that requires medical care. People with depression have an increased risk of suicide. Untreated, depression can be devastating for those who have it and for their families. Fortunately, depression can be treated. With treatment, most people with depression can manage it and get better.

Symptoms of Depression

People with depression may have different symptoms, ranging from mild to severe. However, most people with depression experience changes in mood that impact how they function on a daily basis. People with depression may experience a lack of interest and pleasure in things they previously enjoyed. They may notice changes in sleep patterns, such as staying up all night or having trouble getting out of bed in the morning. They may lack energy, gain or lose weight, or have difficulty concentrating. They may also have feelings of worthlessness, hopelessness, or excessive guilt. Some may feel like life is no longer worth living. Some are tearful or overly emotional. Other common symptoms include a lack of concentration, changes in movement (such as less activity), physical aches and pains, and fatigue. The most serious symptom is suicidal thoughts.

> "I felt like I was failing at life and didn't want to look weak, so I kept struggling through each day without reaching out."[9]
>
> —Joshua Beharry, depression sufferer

The symptoms of depression may arise slowly, beginning with shifts in mood or increased irritability. Joshua Beharry's experience with depression began in 2009. Beharry's first symptoms of depression included increased stress and decreased concentration and energy levels. Beharry says, "I felt like I was failing at life and didn't want to look weak, so I kept struggling through each day without reaching out."[9] Beharry eventually reached out for help and received treatment.

Symptoms may last for a period of a few weeks or for a long time, even years. Because the symptoms may arise slowly, some people may not even notice them. Family members or close friends may notice the symptoms first.

Risk Factors for Anxiety and Depression

Researchers are finding that both genetic and environmental factors contribute to the risk of developing anxiety and depression. Some risk factors—including life events, genetics, and medical conditions—have been identified by researchers. However, there may be other factors that are not yet known.

Specific phobias are common anxiety disorders affecting approximately 8 percent of adults each year. Common phobias include fear of animals (zoophobia), fear of heights (acrophobia), and fear of thunderstorms (astraphobia or brontophobia). People with specific phobias avoid their feared situations or objects. If their feared situation or object is encountered, they experience great distress. Sometimes they may have a panic attack.

Some people have an intense fear of needles. Amanda Walker, a fourth-year medical student at Thomas Jefferson University in Philadelphia, has needle phobia. Her phobia makes getting vaccines and routine injections quite difficult. "I'll start to get really clammy, and then get cold sweats," she says, describing what happens before receiving an injection or vaccine. "Then I pass out." According to the CDC, approximately 7 percent of adults avoid immunizations because of a fear of needles.

Many people with specific phobias recognize that their fear is excessive. Despite that recognition, they are often unable to overcome their fear on their own.

Quoted in Jen Rose Smith, "Millions Have a Real Fear of Needles. Overcoming That Is Critical for Vaccine Rollout," CNN, January 13, 2021. https://edition.cnn.com.

Some of the most common risk factors include trauma, genetics, and alcohol and drug abuse. The presence of these factors does not necessarily mean that someone will develop anxiety or depression. Also, researchers have not definitively ranked these risk factors in order of importance. Simply being aware of them, however, may assist in understanding and diagnosing these disorders. In many cases, doctors are unable to trace anxiety or depression to a single factor or cause.

Suffering from a traumatic event can be a risk factor for anxiety and depression. Childhood sexual abuse, violence, and combat are some examples of traumatic events that may place a person at higher risk for developing these disorders. A 2013 study published in the medical journal *PLOS ONE* identified traumatic events as the

Depression in Older Adults

Although depression is common among older adults, it is not a normal part of aging. In fact, most studies show that older adults are generally satisfied with their lives. Some estimates indicate that 1 to 5 percent of the general older adult population has major depression. The estimates increase to 11.5 percent for older adults who are hospitalized and to 13.5 percent for older adults who have home health care.

Social isolation may increase as a person ages. During the COVID-19 pandemic, many older adults have been isolated from their loved ones due to protective measures. As a result, mental health professionals and caregivers have been concerned by the impact of social isolation on the mental health of older adults.

Older adults with depression may experience different symptoms than do younger people with depression. For some older adults, sadness is not the main symptom of their depression. Instead, they may show a lack of interest in activities they previously enjoyed or may seem numb. They may be less open to expressing their feelings than they were previously. Also, people who experienced depression when they were younger may be more likely to suffer from depression later in life.

biggest cause of anxiety and depression. Professor Peter Kinderman, one of the study's researchers, emphasizes, however, that "the way a person thinks about, and deals with, stressful events is as much an indicator of the level of stress and anxiety they feel."[10]

Genetics is also a risk factor. Researchers are still learning about the genetic factors related to anxiety and depression. Although there is no known anxiety gene, someone is more likely to develop an anxiety disorder if a biological relative has an anxiety disorder or other mental illness. The same is true for depression. If someone has a parent or sibling with major depression, that person probably has a two to three times greater risk of developing depression than someone without that family history. As genetic research advances, scientists will likely continue to explore whether certain genes influence anxiety, depression, and other mental illnesses.

Major life transitions can drastically alter a person's life or daily routines. Getting a divorce, losing a loved one, and moving can cause anxiety and depression. Even seemingly positive life transitions such as marriage and getting a new job can create challenges and stress that may lead to anxiety and depression.

Having a serious illness or disease may cause anxiety and depression due to uncertainty, worry, or sadness about treatment or the future. After suffering a stroke at age thirty-two, Kaitlyn Fieseler struggled with depression. Fieseler says, "I spent the days sobbing and grieving the 'old me' from before the stroke. I wanted to give up."[11] Fieseler received treatment for depression and now volunteers with an organization that helps stroke survivors.

Abusing drugs and alcohol can cause or worsen anxiety and depression, as can withdrawal from these substances. People who are addicted to drugs or alcohol are often diagnosed with anxiety or depression. When a person recognizes their addiction, it can lead to anxiety and depression. Also, as the substances are withdrawn, anxiety and depression may move in. Sometimes people who are anxious or depressed turn to drugs or alcohol in an attempt to soothe symptoms of the disorder.

Aaron Sternlicht, a licensed mental health counselor, explains the connection between substance abuse and anxiety and depression. "Since alcohol and drugs release feel-good neurotransmitters in the brain, they can help numb unpleasant emotions and release feelings of euphoria." He warns that "unfortunately, using substances to cope with depression is a short-term solution that ends up with long-term consequences. As the individual becomes increasingly dependent on the substance, their low mood actually can exacerbate."[12]

> "Unfortunately, using substances to cope with depression is a short-term solution that ends up with long-term consequences. As the individual becomes increasingly dependent on the substance, their low mood actually can exacerbate."[12]
>
> —Aaron Sternlicht, mental health counselor

Sex and Gender

More women experience anxiety and depression than do men. Women are nearly twice as likely as men to be diagnosed with an anxiety disorder in their lifetime. According to a 2018 CDC report, about 10 percent of women in the United States have depression, compared to 5.5 percent of men. The reason why more women experience anxiety and depression is not entirely clear. Some theories relate to differences in brain chemistry and hormone fluctuations, life circumstances and social stressors, and pregnancy and motherhood. For example, the menstrual cycle causes hormonal fluctuations that may affect anxiety and

Research indicates that LGBTQ students suffer from anxiety and depression at more than twice the rate of straight students.

depression. Also, postpartum depression may be experienced after giving birth. Gender inequality and cultural expectations regarding gender roles may also be responsible for the increased prevalence of anxiety and depression in women. Also, women are more likely to be a victim of sexual abuse, which increases the likelihood of having depression.

Some recent studies have highlighted the fact that concerns about gender and sexual identity can cause anxiety or depression. According to Sarah Hayes Skelton and David Pantalone, both of whom are professors and researchers in the psychology department at the University of Massachusetts, Boston, "Anxiety and depression in sexual minority individuals appear to be more than double those of their heterosexual counterparts."[13] Bisexual people may experience anxiety at a higher rate than gay and lesbian people. Researchers have suggested that exclusion from heterosexual or homosexual social groups may be one underlying cause. For transgender people, gender dysphoria, stigma, and marginalization may also cause anxiety or depression.

A series of stressful events can also cause anxiety and depression. Interestingly, having depression is a risk factor for anxiety, and having anxiety is a risk factor for depression. Having low self-esteem has also been shown to be associated with anxiety and depression. Some studies have found that lower levels of income are associated with higher levels of anxiety and depression. Also, some prescription medications may cause anxiety or depression.

In sum, no one factor is responsible for anxiety or depression. These are complex disorders impacted by a variety of factors that scientists are learning more about every day.

CHAPTER TWO

Rising Anxiety and Depression

Prior to the start of the COVID-19 pandemic in 2020, many reports indicated that anxiety and depression were on the rise. A 2018 study published in the *Journal of Psychiatric Research* compared anxiety rates from 2008 to 2018. It revealed an increase in anxiety among adults in the United States, with the largest increase occurring in young adults aged eighteen to twenty-five. A study, this one published in the *Journal of Abnormal Psychology* in 2019, analyzed data from the National Survey on Drug Use and Health. It found that depression increased from 2009 to 2017 among young adults in the United States. In 2009, 8.1 percent of young adults reported symptoms of depression; in 2017, 13.2 percent of them reported such symptoms. The same study found that depression is also on the rise in teens. In 2005, 8.7 percent of teens aged twelve to seventeen reported symptoms of depression; in 2017, 13.2 percent of them reported such symptoms. Teens are aware that anxiety and depression are affecting them as a group. In 2019 the Pew Research Center released a report indicating that 70 percent of teens view anxiety and depression as major problems among their peers.

No one factor explains the increase in anxiety and depression. A variety of factors is likely responsible for the increased prevalence, and those factors may differ by age group and life circumstances. Recently, the pandemic fueled anxiety and depression. New cases of anxiety and depression were reported. For people already living with anxiety and depression, the pandemic tended to increase the severity of symptoms. More than 41 percent of people surveyed by the US Census Bureau reported symptoms of anxiety or depression in January 2021, up from 10.8 percent in January 2019. Studies throughout the world report similar increases in anxiety and depression during the pandemic. Some scientists attribute the pandemic-related increases to social isolation, fear of illness, and lockdowns.

In addition to the pandemic itself, economic, political, and social factors are likely responsible for increasing anxiety and depression. However, the accumulation of a variety of factors is likely to blame for the increase in anxiety and depression.

Pandemic–Fueled Anxiety and Depression

There is no denying that the world is experiencing stressful times. Between the COVID-19 pandemic, climate change, and political and social unrest, the future seems uncertain at times.

According to World Health Organization (WHO) director general Tedros Adhanom Ghebreyesus, the pandemic has caused "mass trauma, which is beyond proportion, even bigger than what the world experienced after the Second World War."[14] The mental health effects of the pandemic are predicted to last for years after it ends. Maria Van Kerkhove, head of the WHO's emerging diseases and zoonosis unit, acknowledges that people have been impacted by the pandemic in different ways. "There are variations in terms of the impact that this has had on individuals, whether you have lost a loved one, or a family member or friend to this virus. Whether you've lost your job, children who haven't been in school, people who are forced to stay home in very difficult situations."[15]

COVID-19 itself is scary. Fear of contracting coronavirus or fear of losing a loved one to COVID-19 can cause anxiety and depression. Actually losing a loved one can also produce symptoms of anxiety and depression. Having COVID-19, like having any serious illness, can trigger anxiety and depression in patients. This may be particularly true for those suffering with lingering symptoms of the disease long after the initial infection, which is generally known as long-haul COVID. Not knowing why some patients have long-lasting symptoms can lead to frustration, confusion, and sadness, which may evolve into anxiety or depression. Those who recover from COVID-19 may also be at risk of developing anxiety or depression. According to Dr. Lakshmi Yatham, head of the department of psychiatry at the University of British Columbia, "There is emerging research showing that if you are diagnosed with COVID-19, your chance of developing symptoms of a mental disorder—ranging from depression and anxiety through to post-traumatic stress disorder—is almost as high as 40 per cent."[16]

A Los Angeles resident gets vaccinated for COVID-19. Some people have anxiety about getting the vaccine due to how quickly it was developed.

The COVID-19 vaccines provoke fear and stress in some people. Some people worry about the safety or effectiveness of the vaccines, given that they were developed quickly. Concerns around reported side effects or fears after experiencing side effects may produce anxiety. In fact, some of the side effects reported at vaccination sites have been blamed on anxiety, not the vaccines themselves.

Even the uncertainty of the duration of the pandemic can cause people to become anxious and depressed. When a new variant is reported or cases surge after a decline, symptoms of anxiety and depression may ramp up too.

Restrictions and Reopening

The various health restrictions—such as lockdowns, quarantine, social distancing, and business and school closures—have resulted in reduced social interactions and even social isolation. At-risk individuals, people who live alone, and older adults have often experienced significant social isolation. Because people depend on others for companionship and emotional support, mental health can decline during social isolation. Loneliness can increase symptoms of depression, and the lack of a support system can exacerbate these symptoms.

Interestingly, when some of the initial restrictions were lifted and places opened up, some people experienced anxiety about returning to normal activities and socializing. Although this has been termed "reopening anxiety" in several news articles, psychiatrist Arthur Bregman refers to this as "cave syndrome."[17] Bregman has seen patients who are afraid to socialize again, and some patients have said they forgot how to do it. He says that some people have cave syndrome due to panic, anxiety, or other disorders.

Inger Burnett-Zeigler, associate professor of psychiatry and psychology at the Feinberg School of Medicine at Northwestern University, explains that some level of anxiety related to reopening is normal. "It's not unusual for people to have difficulty with transition; that's what we noticed at the start of COVID and that's what we'll feel as we transition back to the reentry phase."[18] Burnett-Zeigler cautioned that when the anxiety interferes with work life or relationships or is accompanied by physical symptoms, it is time to seek professional help.

Financial Hardship

The economic impact of the pandemic has also affected the prevalence of anxiety and depression. When businesses closed, particularly in the early stages of the pandemic, many people lost their jobs, either temporarily or permanently. In 2020 over 30 million workers collected unemployment benefits in the United States. Internationally, approximately 400 million were unemployed during 2020. Others have been forced to work fewer hours, resulting in a reduction of income. Many individuals and families have had trouble paying bills. Financial and economic stress can negatively impact mental health. According to the Kaiser Family Foundation, during 2020, 53 percent of adults in households that experienced a job loss or a reduction in income reported symptoms of mental illness, including anxiety and depression, whereas only 32 percent of adults without a loss of job or income in the household reported such symptoms.

"It's not unusual for people to have difficulty with transition; that's what we noticed at the start of COVID and that's what we'll feel as we transition back to the reentry phase."[18]

—Inger Burnett-Zeigler, associate professor of psychiatry and psychology at the Feinberg School of Medicine at Northwestern University

Studies from prior economic downturns confirm that job loss is associated with increased anxiety and depression. Job loss can threaten someone's survival in terms of housing, food, and health care. It can also cause distress and decreased life satisfaction. Carl Van Horn, a professor of public policy at Rutgers University, explains that "losing a job and being unemployed for a long period of time is a psychological trauma and a financial trauma, and the

Climate change has become a source of anxiety and depression for some people. People within the mental health field have recognized climate change as a mental health challenge. Recent studies have shown that an increasing number of people are anxious about the changing planet. According to a 2020 survey conducted by Yale University and George Mason University, four in ten people in the United States felt disgusted or helpless about climate change. A 2019 survey conducted by the American Psychological Association also found that 68 percent of Americans have at least a little eco-anxiety, defined as any anxiety or worry about climate change and its effects. Although eco-anxiety is not a formally recognized anxiety disorder, therapists are reporting more patients worrying about the environment.

Eco-anxiety may be the result of extreme weather events and conditions, such as powerful hurricanes, excessive rainfall, droughts, and wildfires. From 2009 to 2020, the percentage of people in the United States who reported experiencing the effects of climate change increased from 32 percent to 42 percent. Young people seem particularly anxious about the planet—which makes sense, given that they are more likely to endure the consequences of climate change.

two are closely intertwined."[19] Although he recognizes that mental health professionals cannot remedy the economic problem, they can assist people in learning to cope and manage it.

Too Much News

Many people have been glued to the news during the pandemic. Constant consumption of pandemic-related news, such as case counts and ever-changing restrictions, has likely increased anxiety. Psychotherapist Steven Stosny developed a term to describe the anxiety that some people experience when overconsuming the news: headline stress disorder. Although it is not a formally recognized anxiety disorder, headline stress disorder describes a heightened emotional response to constantly reading or watching the news, such as feeling anxious and stressed. The constant anxiety or stress may cause physical symptoms, including chest tightness, heart palpitations, and insomnia, and it may possibly lead to anxiety and depressive disorders.

Studies examining news consumption after past traumas, such as 9/11 and the Boston Marathon bombing, indicate that spending more time watching the news after such events is associated with higher levels of stress. It is also associated with increased onset of new physical health conditions, such as heart problems, several years after the event.

Racial and Ethnic Minorities

According to data from the Kaiser Family Foundation, Black and Hispanic adults have been more likely than White adults to report symptoms of anxiety or depression during the pandemic. In terms of disease-related factors, this is likely due to disproportionately high rates of COVID-19 infection, hospitalization, and death for Black and Hispanic adults. In addition, based on data from the first few months of the pandemic, the financial stress of the pandemic has disproportionately affected Black and Hispanic individuals in the United States. According to a study commissioned by the American Staffing Association, Black and Hispanic respondents were more worried about employment than White respondents in 2020. The study also confirmed that they were more concerned about meeting their financial obligations, such as rent or mortgage payments, student loan debts, and child care costs.

Anti-Asian racism and hate crimes fueled by the pandemic have also contributed to increased anxiety and depression. According to one survey, one in three Asian Americans reported increased symptoms of anxiety and depression during the pandemic. Almost seven out of ten Asian Americans reported that they or their family members experienced some form of discrimination during the first three months of the pandemic. As of May 2021, Stop AAPI Hate had recorded more than sixty-six hundred such incidents since March 2020. Stop AAPI Hate is a coalition

People in New York City gather to protest an upsurge in hate crimes against members of the Asian American community. The Chinese origins of the COVID-19 pandemic led many people to blame Asian people for the pandemic.

that tracks incidents of racism, violence, harassment, and discrimination against Asian Americans and Pacific Islanders in the United States. In a follow-up survey of Asian Americans who reported an incident to the coalition, 20 percent of them had symptoms of racial trauma, such as hypervigilance, intrusive thoughts, and decreased self-esteem.

Young Adults

Young adults have been particularly impacted by the pandemic. They have endured university closures and loss of income, which have likely contributed to poor mental health. The CDC highlighted that young adults (ages eighteen to twenty-four) are more likely to exhibit symptoms of mental health problems during the pandemic than any other age group. During 2020 two-thirds of young adults reported symptoms of anxiety or depression. Young adults were more likely to report new or increased substance use than all adults in 2020. They were also more likely

Technology is an integral part of modern life. Many aspects of life are dependent on technology. When technology fails, it can cause stress and frustration. Worrying about the possibility of it failing can also cause anxiety.

When the pandemic forced people to work and attend school from home, society became even more dependent on technology and internet connectivity. Cile Montgomery, customer experience lead at Dell Technologies, notes, "We are more reliant than ever on our computers to engage with the outside world. Bad technology only isolates us further, adding to an already stressful situation."

A 2021 study published in *Frontiers in Sociology* showed that older adults who used technology to communicate and stay connected during the first year of the pandemic were more stressed and depressed than those who did not. The results contradicted the expectation that technology would help ease social isolation for older adults. Those who were unfamiliar with technology were stressed out. However, those who were familiar with technology were even more stressed out, which surprised researchers.

Quoted in Cathy Cassata, "Tech Issues Stressing You Out During the Pandemic? You're Not Alone," Healthline, April 12, 2021. www.healthline.com.

to report suicidal thoughts; 24 percent of young adults reported recent suicidal thoughts in 2020, whereas 11 percent of all adults reported such thoughts.

The period of young adulthood often involves decisions about colleges, careers, families, relationships, and living environments. It is generally a transition period filled with uncertainty. Dr. Shekhar Saxena, a professor at the Harvard T.H. Chan School of Public Health, explains, "There is the uncertainty of where and what tomorrow will bring, which is faced much more by younger adults than by middle-aged or older adults, because this is the time for change in their lives."[20] The pandemic has likely amplified such uncertainty and may have required young adults to reconsider their plans. Also, young adults were very lonely during the first year of the pandemic. In a survey conducted by researchers at Making Caring Common in October 2020, 61 percent of young adults reported serious loneliness, which was larger than any other age group.

Parenting Challenges

New mothers have also experienced increased anxiety and depression during the pandemic. According to a 2020 study conducted by researchers from the University of Alberta, Canada, 72 percent of new mothers reported experiencing anxiety and 41 percent reported experiencing depression during 2020. This is almost triple the numbers from the pre-pandemic period. Some researchers attribute this to the lack of access to healthcare and social support, as well as increased fears associated with COVID-19 itself.

Also, many parents with children had to quickly learn to balance work and schooling responsibilities from home, which may have contributed to increased reports of anxiety and depression. In a study conducted in June 2020 and published in *Pediatrics*, 27 percent of parents surveyed reported worsening mental health since March 2020.

Health Care Workers

Health care workers have also reported increased symptoms of anxiety and depression during the pandemic. A survey conducted by the University of California, San Francisco, found that half of emergency room workers and first responders experienced high levels of anxiety, burnout, and emotional exhaustion in the summer of 2020. A 2021 study published in *PLOS ONE* that reviewed studies conducted across twenty-one countries found that during the pandemic, one in five health care workers has experienced anxiety, depression, or post-traumatic stress disorder (PTSD).

Several factors help explain the high levels of mental and emotional distress. Working long hours under difficult physical and emotional conditions is likely to blame. The number of patient deaths is another potential reason. Nurses describe experiencing compassion fatigue, which is a condition of overwhelming stress and exhaustion resulting from helping others in need. Emergency physician and CNN medical analyst Leana Wen described front-line workers as "running a marathon at sprint speed, with no end in sight."[21] All health care workers, from ambulance drivers to nurses, respiratory therapists, and doctors, have likely experienced conditions during the pandemic that could trigger anxiety or depression.

Other Major Events Fuel Anxiety and Depression

The pandemic coincided with other major events, which have been reported as increasing anxiety and depression. After George Floyd was killed by police officers in May 2020, anxiety and depression spiked in Black Americans. Among other reasons, this may be due to increased fears of racial violence or reliving past trauma of racial violence. During the week after the video of Floyd's death was released, the number of Black Americans reporting symptoms of anxiety or depression increased from 36 percent to 41 percent, according to US Census Bureau data. Participating in protests of racial violence may have also triggered these symptoms. For example, Tiara Johnson, who has written about mental health issues experienced by the Black community in 2020, experienced a panic attack after participating in a protest over police killings of George Floyd and Breonna Taylor. Johnson says, "Not even five minutes into joining the protest, I began experiencing shortness of breath and sweats, and I could feel [my] heart beating uncontrollably."[22]

> "Not even five minutes into joining the protest, I began experiencing shortness of breath and sweats, and I could feel [my] heart beating uncontrollably."[22]
>
> —Tiara Johnson, protester with panic attacks

A young Black woman confronts police standing guard at a public protest inspired by the May 2020 murder of George Floyd. Some protesters at such rallies have reported symptoms of acute anxiety, including sweating, quickened heartbeat, and shortness of breath.

Another major event in 2020 was the US presidential election. In a 2020 survey conducted on behalf of the American Psychological Association, 68 percent of respondents identified the election as a significant stressor, which was higher than the 2016 election (52 percent). Afton Kapuscinski, director of the Psychological Services Center at Syracuse University, provided his perspective about the feelings that preceded the election. "People believe that the outcome of this election is going to have a serious effect on their lives, and I think beyond that, on their safety. [Voters are] concerned that some of the things that they hold most meaningful are threatened. Although the specific concerns do differ based on political leaning, the feelings that are coming up don't."[23]

The recent accumulation of stressors, particularly in 2020, has greatly impacted mental health and triggered an increase in anxiety and depression. Uncertainty about the future continues to fuel both.

CHAPTER THREE

Teens Struggle with Anxiety and Depression

Dylan Buckner was an Illinois high school senior with a strong academic record. He was also an accomplished football player. As a star quarterback, he had fourteen offers from colleges to play football. His top choice for college was the Massachusetts Institute of Technology. However, on January 7, 2021, he took his own life. Buckner had depression. His parents said that his depression, which appeared several years earlier, had increased during the pandemic. Buckner's depression seemed to worsen after the closure of his school, where he thrived. The activities he participated in outside of school, such as mentoring students with special needs, also disappeared during the pandemic. When Buckner's parents recognized that his depression was worsening in the summer of 2020, they took him to a psychiatrist right away. Buckner started taking antidepressants and received therapy. His parents were stunned by his death, as were his classmates. They had seen him on Zoom in their remote class one hour before his death. Buckner's father believes that his son's brain chemistry made him susceptible to depression but that the pandemic fueled it. Buckner's father said, "Covid's not just killing people by the disease. It's killing people by depression and suicide."[24] Buckner's parents want others to know his story in order to save other teens who might be struggling.

How Teens Experience Anxiety and Depression

Not all teens experience anxiety in the same way. Teens may experience excessive fears and worries, restlessness, and nervousness. Many teens who experience anxiety are concerned with their body image and social acceptance. When teens feel particularly anxious, they may appear overly shy or withdrawn. They may also avoid their usual activities or refuse to engage in new experiences. Some teens may start performing poorly in school or even stop attending school. They may complain when they are not with their friends or assert their need for independence. Some teens turn to risky behaviors, including experimenting with drugs and alcohol or engaging in impulsive sexual behavior. These behaviors may be an attempt to reduce or escape their fears and worries. Teens with excessive anxiety may experience physical symptoms as well. Some teens may report chest pain, stomachaches, muscle pain, headaches, and fatigue. They may also hyperventilate, tremble, flush, or sweat.

"Covid's not just killing people by the disease. It's killing people by depression and suicide."[24]

—Chris Buckner, father of Dylan Buckner, who took his own life during the pandemic

Teens with depression may experience similar symptoms. One early symptom may be irritability. Teens may spend less time with friends or participating in extracurricular activities. They may gain or lose weight, feel tired, and have trouble concentrating. They may also believe that everything is their fault and care less about performing well in school. Some teens may feel like life is not worth living. Physical symptoms include frequent headaches and stomachaches. The symptoms may arise after an event, such as the death of a loved one, or appear out of nowhere.

Trends in Anxiety and Depression in Teens

According to most reports, anxiety and depression are on the rise in teens. This trend was occurring even before the pandemic, which created more mental health challenges for teens. According to the National Survey of Children's Health, researchers found a 20 percent increase in children and teens (aged six to seventeen) diagnosed with anxiety from 2007 to 2012. As of 2016, over 10 percent of teens were diagnosed with an anxiety disorder. Of course, that number does not reflect cases of teen anxiety that are undiagnosed. According to Dr. Richa Bhatia, spokesperson for the Anxiety and Depression Association of America, anxiety disorders affect approximately 15 to 30 percent of teens in the United States. A CDC report showed that more teens experienced persistent feelings of sadness or hopelessness in 2019 (36.7 percent) than in 2009 (26.1 percent).

Teen girls are especially prone to developing anxiety and depression. According to various studies, teen girls are two to three times as likely as teen boys to experience anxiety and depression. Teen girls are also more likely than teen boys to attempt suicide, although teen boys are more likely to die by suicide. However, according to a study published in *JAMA Network Open*, the gap between male and female teen suicide death rates has narrowed over the past decades.

Suicide rates have actually been increasing over time. A CDC report showed that more teens attempted suicide in 2019 (8.9 percent) than in 2009 (6.3 percent). Also, the suicide rate for those aged ten to twenty-four increased 56 percent from 2007 to 2017, according to the CDC. Forty-two states experienced an increase in youth and young adult suicide rates from 2007–2009 to 2016–2018.

Troubling Trends in Teen Mental Health and Suicide

Experts have identified a troubling picture in mental health and suicide trends among US high school students. National surveys conducted between 2009 and 2019 reveal rising numbers of students who report persistent feelings of sadness or hopelessness. Those same surveys also show an increase in students reporting suicidal thoughts and behaviors. The survey results, described in a 2020 report by the Centers for Disease Control and Prevention, do not take into account the additional stresses brought on by the pandemic.

The percentage of high school students who:	2009 Total	2011 Total	2013 Total	2015 Total	2017 Total	2019 Total
Experienced persistent feelings of sadness or hopelessness	26.1%	28.5%	29.9%	29.9%	31.5%	36.7%
Seriously considered attempting suicide	13.8%	15.8%	17%	17.7%	17.2%	18.8%
Made a suicide plan	10.9%	12.8%	13.6%	14.6%	13.6%	15.7%
Attempted suicide	6.3%	7.8%	8%	8.6%	7.4%	8.9%
Were injured in a suicide attempt that had to be treated by a doctor or nurse	1.9%	2.4%	2.7%	2.8%	2.4%	2.5%

Source: "Youth Risk Behavior Survey Data Summary & Trends Report 2009–2019," Centers for Disease Control and Prevention, 2020. www.cdc.gov.

Some researchers caution that the increase in anxiety and depression rates may be due to increased awareness, although that does not explain increasing rates of suicide. Dr. John T. Walkup, chair of the department of psychiatry at Lurie Children's Hospital of Chicago, explained, "If you look at past studies, you don't know if the conditions themselves are increasing or clinicians are making the diagnosis more frequently due to advocacy or public health efforts."[25] Nevertheless, the prevalence of anxiety and depression among teens is concerning.

It is critical that teens with anxiety and depression obtain treatment. If anxiety disorders are not treated, teens are at risk of poor

School shootings are an unfortunate reality and can cause anxiety for teens. Being exposed to a school shooting can cause trauma, which can trigger anxiety, depression, and PTSD. In addition, school shootings can cause worry and anxiety for teens who learn about the shootings from the news or social media.

Following the shooting at Marjory Stoneman Douglas High School in Parkland, Florida, in 2018, a Pew Research Center survey showed that a majority (57 percent) of teens were worried about a shooting at their own school. One in four teens said that they were "very worried."

Worry can even arise during active-shooter drills. Em Odesser describes her thoughts during such a drill when she was a high school senior living in Westchester, New York: "This would be my only protection against someone who was trying to murder me: A desk. A door. A dark closet."

Quoted in Claire Lampen, "Living in Fear of Mass Shootings Is Giving Students PTSD," *Teen Vogue*, May 24, 2018. www.teenvogue.com.

academic performance, impaired relationships, and substance abuse. Teens with untreated depression are at higher risk of self-harm, substance abuse, and suicide. They are even more likely to develop other diseases later in life, such as heart, kidney, and liver disease.

Pandemic Impacts Teen Anxiety and Depression

Anxiety and depression have increased in teens during the pandemic. Teens' ability to socialize has been severely impacted during the pandemic, which is one likely source of increased anxiety and depression. According to John MacPhee, executive director and chief executive officer (CEO) of the Jed Foundation, a nonprofit that seeks to increase mental health support programs in schools, lack of socialization has been detrimental to teens. "They're wired to be with other people, to be separating their identity from their parents. It's very, very important for their identity, and this pandemic has really interrupted and insulted that."[26]

There have been mixed reports about whether suicide and suicide attempts have increased during the pandemic. Some data indicate an increase in suicide rates in teens, at least at certain time periods during the pandemic. According to CDC data, during May 2020, emergency room visits involving suspected suicide attempts increased in teens aged twelve to seventeen. During a one-month period in early 2021, there was a 51 percent increase in those visits for girls compared with the same period in 2019. For boys, the increase was about 4 percent.

The CDC speculated that young people were at higher risk of suicide during the first year of the pandemic due to physical distancing and lack of connectedness to schools, teachers, and peers. Other reasons cited were the cancellation of activities, lack of access to mental health treatment, increase in substance use, and anxiety about family health and economic problems. Some teens may have felt cheated when forced to miss out on anticipated school activities like prom, school trips, or graduation. Many teens depend on school resources for their mental health needs. Without that safety net, many schools feared that students were not receiving the care they needed.

> "They're wired to be with other people, to be separating their identity from their parents. It's very, very important for their identity, and this pandemic has really interrupted and insulted that."[26]
>
> —John MacPhee, executive director and CEO of the Jed Foundation

For Catherine Zorn, the beginning of the pandemic was particularly challenging. Although she has had suicidal thoughts and panic attacks since middle school, the closure of her dance school in March 2020 triggered troubling thoughts and feelings. As a seventeen-year-old ballerina, she found peace at the dance studio. Without it, Zorn's anxiety and depression took over. She engaged in self-harm and even considered ending her life. Zorn explained, "I didn't see a way out of the feelings and thoughts I was having."[27] She asked for help and obtained inpatient treatment. Zorn is one of many teens to seek emergency treatment for suicidal thoughts during the pandemic.

Mental health concerns have been cited as a reason to reopen schools and after-school activities. However, even as schools reopen for in-person learning and activities resume, student quarantine orders and temporary school closures due to an outbreak are causing ongoing anxiety. Given the uncertainty of the pandemic, the full extent of its impact on teen mental health is unknown.

Social Acceptance

In addition to the pandemic, a variety of other factors has been blamed for rising anxiety and depression in teens. Pressures to fit in socially and to perform well academically are commonly cited as potential causes for the increase. Attention has also been paid to the impact of social media on teens' mental health.

Many teens strive to be accepted socially. This desire is not unique to teens, but the school environment is a unique setting in which being accepted by peers feels particularly important. A 2019 report by the Pew Research Center indicated that three out of ten teens reported a lot of pressure to look good (29 percent) and fit in socially (28 percent). The desire to fit in can become a source of anxiety and depression, especially if behaviors are modified or activities are avoided.

Being rejected socially can also increase anxiety and depression. According to C. Nathan DeWall, a psychologist at the University of Kentucky, "Humans have a fundamental need to belong. Just as we have needs for food and water, we also have needs for positive and lasting relationships."[28] It is important to recognize that everyone experiences social rejection at times. DeWall recommends talking through the feelings surrounding rejection in order to move past them.

Academic Pressure

Academic pressure is another reason cited by experts for the increase in teen anxiety and depression. According to a 2019 report by the Pew Research Center, six out of ten teens (61 percent) said they personally felt a lot of pressure to earn good grades. A 2018 study by the Better Sleep Council reported that 74 percent of teens are stressed out because of homework. Increased competition can be a source of motivation for some students. However, too much competition can cause some students to become anxious or depressed. Academic pressure can come from outsiders, such as parents and teachers, or from the teens themselves. Teens' own expectations, which may be influenced by societal expectations, can make strong academic performance seem vital for survival into adulthood. Intensely focusing on college can be a source of the problem too. Teens are worried not only about getting into college but also about paying for it. For many teens, the high costs of college make attendance impossible without the

Medical experts have cited academic pressure, including pressure to do well on major exams, as one of the triggers of severe anxiety and depression in teenagers.

help of financial aid and scholarships, many of which are awarded to students with the highest grades and test scores.

Schools have also become more focused on testing in recent years, partly due to external pressures that are placed on them. When school officials and teachers are stressed out about test scores, students can absorb that stress too.

Teens often juggle academic responsibilities with multiple extracurricular activities, such as sports, art, music, and community service. Many teens work at night and on weekends. Teens' schedules may not leave much time for relaxing, socializing, or even sleep. All of these things may make teens more anxious or depressed.

Social Media

Social media has been blamed for increased anxiety and depression in teens. However, the research results are mixed. A 2018 Pew Research Center survey found that 45 percent of teens aged thirteen to seventeen are online almost constantly, and 97 percent use a social media platform, such as YouTube, Facebook, Instagram, or Snapchat. Social media is used to communicate, to build social networks, for entertainment, and for self-expression. Young people in marginalized communities often find supportive communities online. However, social media may also negatively impact teens. Social media can disrupt sleep, expose teens to bullying, and create unreal expectations or perceptions of others. Some teens may be prone to peer pressure via social media platforms.

Several studies have shown that such negative impacts are linked to the time spent on social media; the risk of mental health problems increased as teens spent more time using social media. One of these is a 2016 study published in the *Journal of Adolescence*. It found that teens who used social media more (overall and at night) and had a higher emotional investment in social media had higher levels of anxiety and depression and poorer sleep

Medical experts point out that some high school students, especially females, suffer from symptoms of anxiety and depression after being repeatedly bullied by their peers.

quality. However, a 2019 study published in *Computers in Human Behavior* found that screen time alone was not directly responsible for increased anxiety and depression. That study followed teens' social media use over an eight-year period. The study's researchers suggested that the way teens use social media may be a more direct influence on anxiety and depression.

Other studies have confirmed that the ways teens use social media is important for mental health. A 2015 study published in the *Journal of Abnormal Child Psychology* found that teens who used social media to seek feedback and make social comparisons were more likely to be depressed than teens who used social media for other purposes.

The majority of teens report feeling positive about the benefits of social media, such as staying connected to friends and family and showcasing their creativity online. In a 2018 Pew Research Center study, 81 percent of teens reported that using social media made them feel more connected to their friends' lives. However,

According to the CDC, suicide is the second leading cause of death among young people aged ten to twenty-four. The risk of suicide is higher for LGBTQ youth than straight and cisgender youth.

According to CDC data from a survey of high school students in 2019, 29 percent of transgender students have attempted suicide, compared to 7 percent of cisgender students. Similarly, 21 percent of gay and lesbian students and 22 percent of bisexual students have attempted suicide, compared to 7 percent of straight students.

In 2020 the Trevor Project conducted a survey of forty thousand LGBTQ people aged thirteen to twenty-four. Of the survey respondents, 68 percent had symptoms of generalized anxiety disorder, 55 percent had symptoms of depression, and 48 percent engaged in self-harm. Fifteen percent reported a suicide attempt within the past year. The research indicates that physical or verbal harassment, abuse, or bullying of LGBTQ people increases the chances of self-harm.

some teens reported negative feelings associated with using social media. The same study found that 45 percent of teens reported that social media made them feel overwhelmed because of all of the drama on these sites. Also, 40 percent of teens felt pressured to only create posts that portray them well or will attract lots of comments or likes. One in four teens reported that social media sites made them feel worse about their life.

Many teens actually turn to social media when they are depressed or anxious. According to a 2018 study by Hopelab, at least 90 percent of teens and young adults with symptoms of depression reported seeking information about mental health online. Some teens, approximately 20 percent, are using messaging, apps, or video chats to connect with a health professional.

Social media is a relatively recent development, with the first social media site (SixDegrees) dating back to 1997. Facebook, Twitter, and YouTube were all started in the early 2000s. As a result, the long-term impacts of social media use on mental health are still unknown. Nevertheless, many mental health professionals recommend limiting the time spent on social media and examining how using social media impacts one's life. If using it is producing negative feelings or thoughts, it may be best to take a break from it or impose time limitations. Some experts recommend limiting nighttime use because it can interfere with sleep, and decreased sleep can increase symptoms of anxiety and depression. "The key messages to young people are: Get enough sleep; don't lose contact with your friends in real life; and physical activity is important for mental health and well-being,"[29] says Dasha Nicholls, head of the Child and Adolescent Mental Health research team at Imperial College London. Nicholls says that if teens take care of themselves in those ways, they should not have to worry about the negative impact of social media.

> "The key messages to young people are: Get enough sleep; don't lose contact with your friends in real life; and physical activity is important for mental health and well-being."[29]
>
> —Dasha Nicholls, head of the Child and Adolescent Mental Health research team at Imperial College London

It is abundantly clear that teens' mental health has been challenged over the past several years. With the ongoing uncertainty, teens will continue to struggle with normal teenage issues as well as pandemic-related concerns. As the pandemic has further highlighted the importance of caring for mental health, teens should feel encouraged and empowered to speak freely about their mental health, including symptoms of anxiety and depression. With professional care and support, teens with these mental illnesses can thrive.

CHAPTER FOUR

Treating Anxiety and Depression

Anxiety and depression are challenging and even debilitating for some people. However, there is a variety of treatment options that allow people to manage these disorders and live full lives. Sometimes a person will be prescribed medication or therapy—or both. The decision as to which treatment is appropriate is based on an individual's needs and preferences as well as the individual's diagnosis and overall health. The length of treatment varies from person to person. Some people may see improvement in a few months, whereas others may require more time to see results.

Medication and therapy are effective for most individuals with anxiety and depression. China McCarney, a former professional baseball player who has panic attacks, found therapy particularly helpful. He says, "Therapy gave me permission to be the 100% true version of myself. I did not have to be ashamed anymore and I realized that it was ok to not be ok sometimes."[30] It is important that the effectiveness of treatment is closely monitored and that medication is taken as directed. Even with treatment, there is a risk of suicide for those with depression, although the risk is lower.

One person with anxiety and panic disorder anonymously described their treatment journey. After experiencing a variety of symptoms, including a panic attack, they turned to doctors for help. Once diagnosed with anxiety and panic disorder, they tried several medications before finding what worked for them. They also educated themselves on the disorders, identified their triggers, and learned techniques to deal with the disorders. They connected with a support group, which many people find helpful because such groups allow people to share experiences and to feel less alone. Since beginning treatment, they report living a full life: "I've gotten married, moved out, bought my first home, adopted two dogs, started a new job and traveled across the country—all with this anxiety disorder by my side."[31]

"Therapy gave me permission to be the 100% true version of myself. I did not have to be ashamed anymore and I realized that it was ok to not be ok sometimes."[30]

—China McCarney, individual with panic attacks

A treatment plan for a person with anxiety, depression, or both is tailored to the individual. However, anxiety and depression can often be treated in similar ways. After ruling out medical and other possible causes for anxiety or depression, treatment plans can include psychotherapy, medications, and complementary health approaches. Safety planning is also critical for people with suicidal thoughts.

Therapy

Psychotherapy—which is also called talk therapy, counseling, or just therapy—with a licensed therapist may be helpful for discussing triggers, reactions, and coping mechanisms. One form of psychotherapy that is an effective treatment method for anxiety and depression is cognitive behavioral therapy (CBT). CBT focuses on identifying unhelpful emotions, thoughts, and behaviors and changing them. CBT encourages patients to challenge unhealthy and distorted thoughts in order to create new, healthy patterns of behavior. It is generally the first treatment option for people with anxiety or depression. Although CBT is a time-limited therapy that typically lasts twelve to sixteen sessions, there is a lot of research to support its long-term effectiveness. According to therapist Mary Heekin, people with anxiety disorders "respond well to CBT's focus on thoughts and behaviors. By identifying automatic thought patterns that lead to a sense of danger, CBT helps people experience fewer and less severe symptoms of dread, anxiety, and panic, and to avoid being controlled by their fear."[32] Between sessions, there is generally homework assigned by the therapist so that patients can practice what they have learned during the sessions. People generally feel in control of their recovery, given that they are actively involved in changing their own thought and behavior patterns. Heekin believes that CBT is different from other approaches because the patient collaborates with the therapist and the therapy is goal oriented.

Acceptance and commitment therapy (ACT) is a mindfulness-based therapy that aims to teach people skills to accept difficult experiences or emotions in a way that leads to changes in behavior and emotions. Instead of denying or avoiding painful emotions or thoughts, with ACT people learn the skills to cope with unpleasant thoughts and feelings, including by reframing them. ACT can be used to treat anxiety and depression.

Interpersonal therapy (IPT) is a short-term psychotherapy that targets interpersonal issues related to depression, such as relationships, family conflict, and social isolation. The initial sessions are aimed at learning about a person's interpersonal experiences and the nature of the person's depression. Later sessions are generally designed to teach strategies to deal with the identified issues. IPT generally consists of twelve to sixteen weekly sessions that last an hour.

Exposure therapy is another type of psychotherapy that is generally used for anxiety when CBT is ineffective. Exposure therapy involves exposing an individual to a feared object or

Research shows that participation in group therapy can be helpful to people suffering from depression because they feel less alone.

situation in order to reduce the fear over time. There are other types of psychotherapy that may be used to treat anxiety and depression. And group therapy is available in addition to individual therapy.

Medication

Medication is generally a safe and effective way to treat anxiety and depression. The four major classes of medications used to treat anxiety are selective serotonin reuptake inhibitors (SSRIs), serotonin-norepinephrine reuptake inhibitors, tricyclic antidepressants, and benzodiazepines. Some of those same medications can also be used to treat depression. Actress Amanda Seyfried takes medication to manage her anxiety. She urges others to use the tools necessary to manage mental illness. "A mental illness is a thing that people cast in a different category [from other illnesses], but I don't think it is. It should be taken as seriously as anything else,"[33] she says.

Medication must be tailored to each individual, and it often takes time to arrive at the proper medication type and dosage. Some medications may take some time before providing any relief, whereas others may provide fast-acting relief but are only intended for short-term use. These medications may cause side effects. For example, possible side effects of SSRIs include drowsiness, weight loss or gain, headache, nausea, and dizziness. People should discuss any side effects with their doctor. Sometimes the medication can be adjusted to eliminate or reduce these issues. In some cases, the doctor may stop the medication under close monitoring. Given the nature of these medications, a doctor should be consulted before discontinuing use or reducing dosage.

Although medications can be helpful, some medications have serious risks, including a risk of suicide. In October 2004 the US Food and Drug Administration (FDA) issued a warning that antidepressant medications, including SSRIs, may increase suicidal thoughts and behavior in children and teens. Although the FDA does not prohibit these medications for children and teens, it requires that manufacturers include a product label—known as a black box warning—to warn patients and families of the risks, which must be balanced against clinical need. A few years later, the FDA extended the warning to include the increased risks of suicidal thinking and behavior in young adults (aged eighteen to twenty-four). Children, teens, and young adults should discuss all concerns about antidepressants and other medications with their doctor, family member, or other responsible adult.

New or Promising Treatment Options

Outside of Western medicine, complementary and alternative medicine provides possible options for treating anxiety and depression. These include mind-body therapies such as meditation, manipulative therapies such as massage, energy therapies such as Reiki, and methods of traditional Chinese medicine.

Complementary medicine is used alongside conventional medicine, and alternative medicine is used instead of conventional medicine.

Some studies have confirmed the effectiveness of complementary and alternative medicine for treating anxiety and depression. For example, yoga and meditation have been used to treat anxiety and depression with some success. Acupuncture, a traditional form of Chinese medicine that involves the insertion of tiny needles along energy lines in the body, has also been shown to reduce anxiety and depression in some instances.

Eye movement desensitization and reprocessing (EMDR) is a relatively new form of psychotherapy used to help people heal from symptoms and emotional distress caused by disturbing life experiences. It was initially developed in 1987 to treat PTSD. EMDR is intended to change how the brain stores a traumatic or painful memory in order to reduce and eliminate

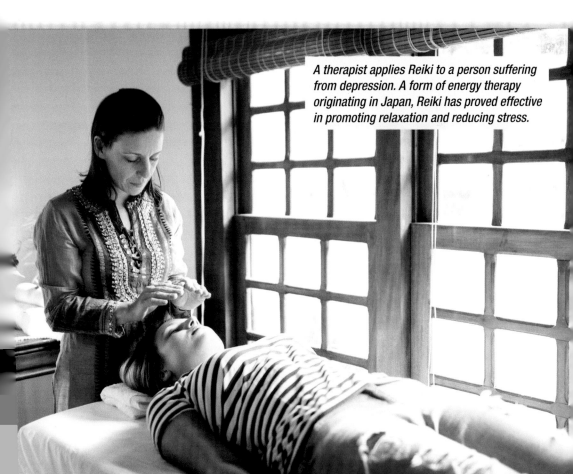

A therapist applies Reiki to a person suffering from depression. A form of energy therapy originating in Japan, Reiki has proved effective in promoting relaxation and reducing stress.

the problematic symptoms associated with it. A typical session requires a patient to briefly recall difficult memories while a therapist directs a patient's eyes to move back and forth, which is intended to divert the patient's attention and make the memory less upsetting. It may also involve tapping on various parts of the body. EMDR may provide benefits in less time than other forms of therapy. Prince Harry uses EMDR to cope with anxiety associated with the death of his mother, Princess Diana. He turned to EMDR after years of traditional behavioral therapy. Harry says, "One of the biggest lessons that I've ever learned in life is you've sometimes got to go back and to deal with really uncomfortable situations and be able to process it in order to be able to heal."[34] Although some people have reported success with EMDR, more research is needed to support its effectiveness in treating anxiety.

> "One of the biggest lessons that I've ever learned in life is you've sometimes got to go back and to deal with really uncomfortable situations and be able to process it in order to be able to heal."[34]
>
> —Prince Harry, who uses EMDR therapy

For depression, brain stimulation therapies can be tried if psychotherapy and medication are not effective. One type of brain stimulation is electroconvulsive therapy (ECT), which involves electrically stimulating the brain while the patient is under general anesthesia. Renowned American composer Paul Moravec credits ECT with helping him recover from depression. He compares his experience with ECT to "rebooting a computer."[35] After his treatment, his improvement was almost immediate. He even won a Pulitzer Prize in music after ECT.

How Technology Can Help

Scientists have been exploring whether virtual reality can ease anxiety, Alzheimer's disease, and chronic pain. Although virtual reality originated in the entertainment and gaming industries, its

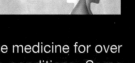

Acupuncture has been used in traditional Chinese medicine for over three thousand years to treat a variety of health conditions. Some people turn to acupuncture to help ease mental health disorders when traditional treatment options are ineffective.

Acupuncture is a technique whereby tiny needles, about the size of a human hair, are pushed into the skin. The placement of the needles depends on the condition being treated. According to Chinese medicine, the body becomes ill when the energy flow within it becomes blocked. The needles are intended to open the energy channels, which is thought to restore health.

Although there is limited research examining the benefits of acupuncture for anxiety and depression, some studies have reported that the symptoms of anxiety and depression are eased with acupuncture treatments. Mental health professionals can advise patients on whether acupuncture may be beneficial and how to find a licensed practitioner. Acupuncture can be risky for people with certain medical conditions, including those who are pregnant or at risk for infection. Because needles are involved, proper sterilization techniques must be performed to prevent infection.

effect on the brain is interesting and is the subject of research. Whether virtual reality is able to quell anxiety and depression is still open to debate, but some therapists are implementing it alongside other treatments. Since the 1990s, virtual reality has been used to treat PTSD, mostly in veterans and soldiers. Now virtual reality is being incorporated into exposure therapy and CBT to treat a variety of anxiety disorders. For example, some therapists are using virtual reality in exposure therapy for people with specific phobic disorders. People can be exposed to a fear, such as flying on a plane, through a virtual reality headset in a therapist's office. The therapist can control the exposure, and it is often quicker and cheaper than exposing the person to the fear in real life. Although its effectiveness is not established, virtual reality may be another tool for mental health treatment.

Mental health care is also moving into the virtual space. Virtual appointments with therapists and doctors have increased since the beginning of the pandemic. People can book an appointment with a therapist or doctor and conduct the session online from the comfort of their home. This may be especially beneficial for people who have limited transportation or live in an area with few mental health providers. Some people may prefer to conduct the therapy session or doctor's appointment from home due to privacy concerns. In fact, people with anxiety or depression may be more willing to conduct a session virtually, especially if going to an office promotes anxiety or if the person has a fear of leaving the house.

In addition, some people are chatting with chatbot therapists, which employ artificial intelligence (AI) to provide comfort and support. Although not an FDA-approved medical treatment, AI therapy may be helpful between appointments with regular therapists. AI therapists may be helpful after hours when access to therapists may be limited. AI therapists may also provide companionship when someone is lonely or feeling sad. AI therapists are limited in the services they can provide—they are not doctors and do not treat patients—and by the algorithms that control them. After all, they are not human.

Online support groups may serve similar purposes. People with anxiety and depression disorders may turn to online support groups when needs arise. Such support groups may help people realize that they are not alone.

Getting Help

Mental health is a vital aspect of overall health. However, not everyone who has anxiety or depression gets treated. According to the Anxiety & Depression Association of America (ADAA), only 36.9 percent of people with an anxiety disorder receive treatment. A 2019 study published in *JAMA Pediatrics* showed that almost half of children and teens in the United States with a mental illness do not receive treatment. The reasons for not seeking or receiv-

In recent years, the general public has begun paying more attention to the importance of mental health. For some people this has made it easier to talk to physicians and other medical professionals about mental health challenges.

ing treatment vary. Some people do not receive treatment due to financial barriers, a shortage of mental health professionals, and stigma. There are also significant disparities in mental health care access among different racial and ethnic groups.

Kellene Diana, a writer, struggled with anxiety and depression for a long time before seeking help. She explains, "Nobody understood or wanted to understand; in fact they called me names and passed judgment before they even knew what I was going through."[36] As a result, she stopped speaking about her struggles for years. Eventually, she stopped worrying about what other people thought and focused on getting better. After acknowledging her struggles, she made an appointment with a therapist. She credits therapy and other techniques, such as prayer and meditation, for her recovery. Like many people who have been treated for mental illness, she encourages others to seek help so that they can control their anxiety and depression.

The growing awareness of the importance of mental health may make it easier to talk about mental health challenges with friends, family, and doctors. People who suspect they have anxiety or depression should seek help from professional providers, such as psychiatrists, therapists, and physicians. It is best to seek help as soon as possible because early diagnosis and intervention generally lead to better treatment results.

With treatment, many people with anxiety and depression get better. It may happen very quickly, or it may take a while after starting treatment. For Adina Young, who was diagnosed with depression in 2000, it took a while after being diagnosed to find what treatment worked. This included opening up about mental illness. Young says, "Now, I am proud to say I have depression and anxiety and proud to say I have a therapist and take 3 different pills."[37] Young has established friendships with people who have battled mental illness, and they often share their daily successes and challenges. As Young confirms, having supportive friends who understand mental illness can help destigmatize it.

Mindfulness

Mindfulness is maintaining awareness of the present moment. Studies have shown that mindfulness can help reduce anxiety and depression. Because the focus is on what is happening now, mindfulness can reduce fears or sadness about the past and the future. It has also been shown to reduce obsessive thoughts (thinking the same thoughts over and over), improve sleep, and decrease burnout.

Some people equate mindfulness with seated meditation. However, seated meditation is only one way to practice mindfulness. Other techniques include breath work and walking meditation. It can be as simple as taking time out for a few seconds to notice one's surroundings. Experimenting with different techniques and exercises can help people discover which works best for them.

Like any treatment option, not everyone benefits from mindfulness. A few recent studies found that some people experienced unwanted effects of meditation, including increased anxiety. However, the overwhelming majority of the research reports positive benefits from mindfulness.

Mental health resources are available in a variety of settings. Schools provide mental health resources for students. Colleges and universities are placing more emphasis on the mental health of their students, and many provide on-campus mental health services. Many employers provide mental health resources as part of employee benefit plans. Professional organizations recognize the mental health challenges of particular professions and often provide support to their members. The internet also provides a lot of information and can connect people with mental health professionals in their community. Given the prevalence of and increase in mental illnesses, including anxiety and depression, mental health services and resources will likely expand to meet the growing need.

"Now, I am proud to say I have depression and anxiety and proud to say I have a therapist and take 3 different pills."[37]

—Adina Young, individual with depression and anxiety

Introduction: Spotlight on Mental Health

1. Quoted in Lipi Roy, "'Lifelong Pal, Anxiety': Why Ryan Reynolds, Naomi Osaka, and Other Celebrities Need to Discuss Mental Health," *Forbes*, June 14, 2021. www.forbes.com.
2. Quoted in Roy, "'Lifelong Pal, Anxiety.'"
3. Naomi Osaka, "It's O.K. Not to Be O.K.," *Time*, July 8, 2021. https://time.com.
4. Quoted in Allison Gordon, "Michelle Obama Says She's Suffering from 'Low-Grade Depression,'" CNN, August 8, 2020. https://edition.cnn.com.
5. Quoted in Jen Christensen, "The Pandemic Has Pushed Children's Mental Health and Access to Care to a 'Crisis Point,'" CNN, July 22, 2021. https://edition.cnn.com.
6. Osaka, "It's O.K. Not to Be O.K."

Chapter One: What Are Anxiety and Depression?

7. Hara Howard, "'Coming Out'—My Journey with Anxiety," Anxiety & Depression Association of America, March 4, 2021. https://adaa.org. (Can be found at web.archive.org.)
8. Ashley Fisher, "Whose Brain Is This Anyway?," Anxiety & Depression Association of America, May 20, 2021. https://adaa.org. (Can be found at web.archive.org.)
9. Joshua Beharry, "Journey to Recovery," Anxiety & Depression Association of America, June 14, 2021. https://adaa.org. (Can be found at web.archive.org.)
10. Quoted in University of Liverpool, "Traumatic Life Events Biggest Cause of Anxiety, Depression," ScienceDaily, October 16, 2013. www.sciencedaily.com.
11. Kaitlyn Fieseler, "My Stroke Story," Anxiety & Depression Association of America, May 3, 2021. https://adaa.org. (Can be found at web.archive.org.)
12. Quoted in Jon McKenna, "How Are Depression and Substance Abuse Related?," WebMD, July 11, 2021. www.webmd.com.

13. Sarah Hayes Skelton and David Pantalone, "Anxiety and Depression in Sexual and Gender Minority Individuals," Anxiety & Depression Association of America, March 6, 2018. https://adaa.org.

Chapter Two: Rising Anxiety and Depression

14. Quoted in Will Feuer, "WHO Says Pandemic Has Caused More 'Mass Trauma' than WWII," CNBC, March 5, 2021. www.cnbc.com.
15. Quoted in Feuer, "WHO Says Pandemic Has Caused More 'Mass Trauma' than WWII."
16. Quoted in University of British Columbia, "Tackling the Science Behind the Long-Term Effects of COVID-19," July 5, 2021. www.med.ubc.ca.
17. Quoted in Anna Russell, "The Age of Reopening Anxiety," *New Yorker*, June 3, 2021. www.newyorker.com.
18. Quoted in Anushree Dave, "Reentry Anxiety: 7 Ways to Deal with Stress About Post-pandemic Life," *Self*, April 23, 2021. www.self.com.
19. Quoted in Stephanie Pappas, "The Toll of Job Loss: The Unemployment and Economic Crises Sparked by COVID-19 Are Expected to Have Far-Reaching Mental Health Impacts," *Monitor on Psychology*, vol. 1, no. 7, 2020. www.apa.org.
20. Quoted in Dana Alkhouri, "Pandemic's Mental Health Burden Heaviest Among Young Adults," ABC News, February 21, 2021. https://abcnews.go.com.
21. Quoted in Megan Marples, "Over 1 in 5 Health Care Workers Experience Depression and Anxiety During the Pandemic, Study Says," CNN, March 11, 2021. https://edition.cnn.com.
22. Tiara Johnson, "Living with 2020 Vision," Anxiety & Depression Association of America, May 3, 2021. https://adaa.org. (Can be found at web.archive.org.)
23. Quoted in Alia E. Dastagir, "Election 2020: Terrified to Lose and Afraid to Hope," *USA Today*, October 28, 2020. www.usatoday.com.

Chapter Three: Teens Struggle with Anxiety and Depression

24. Quoted in Elizabeth Chuck, "Their Teen Killed Himself. Now They Want to Save Others Struggling During the Pandemic," NBC News, February 6, 2021. www.nbcnews.com.
25. Quoted in Amy Ellis Nutt, "Why Kids May Face Far More Anxiety These Days," *Washington Post*, May 10, 2018. www.washingtonpost.com.
26. Quoted in Chuck, "Their Teen Killed Himself."

27. Quoted in Rose Wang, "As COVID-19 Rose, So Did Teen Suicide Attempts. Girls Are at Most Risk," *Houston (TX) Chronicle*, August 4, 2021. www.houstonchronicle.com.
28. Quoted in Kirsten Weir, "The Pain of Social Rejection," *Monitor on Psychology*, vol. 43, no. 4, 2012. www.apa.org.
29. Quoted in Jamie Ducharme, "Social Media Hurts Girls More than Boys," *Time*, August 13, 2019. https://time.com.

Chapter Four: Treating Anxiety and Depression

30. China McCarney, "Mental Illness Warrior," Anxiety & Depression Association of America, May 4, 2021. https://adaa.org. (Can be found at web.archive.org.)
31. Quoted in National Alliance on Mental Illness, "My Journey with Anxiety and Panic Disorder," 2021. www.nami.org.
32. Quoted in Molly Burford, "What Is Cognitive Behavioral Therapy and How Does it Work?," *Allure*, October 16, 2019. www.allure.com.
33. Quoted in David Denicolo, "Amanda Seyfried on Her Mental Health, Her Dog, and Those Eyes," *Allure*, October 18, 2016. www.allure.com.
34. Quoted in Alia E. Dastagir, "Prince Harry Said He Is Triggered Flying into London and Uses EMDR to Cope. What Is It?," *USA Today*, May 21, 2021. www.usatoday.com.
35. Quoted in A. Pawlowski, "Life After Depression: Why So Little Is Known About People Who Go On to Thrive," *Today*, November 12, 2018. www.today.com.
36. Kellene Diana, "I Beat Anxiety and Depression," Anxiety & Depression Association of America, September 7, 2018. https://adaa.org. (Can be found at web.archive.org.)
37. Adina Young, "A Long Line of Depression and Anxiety: The Stigma Stops Here," Anxiety & Depression Association of America, May 22, 2018. https://adaa.org. (Can be found at web.archive.org.)

Centers for Disease Control and Prevention (CDC)

www.cdc.gov

The CDC is the premier public health agency in the United States. Its website includes the latest information about anxiety and depression, including information about children and teens.

National Alliance on Mental Illness (NAMI)

www.nami.org

NAMI is a large grassroots organization that seeks to improve the lives of those living with and affected by mental illness in the United States. Its website provides information as well as ways to connect with mental health professionals and to join online discussion groups.

National Institute of Mental Health (NIMH)

www.nimh.nih.gov

The NIMH is the leading federal agency in the United States that focuses on researching mental illness. Its website provides information on a range of mental health disorders, as well as the latest research.

National Suicide Prevention Lifeline

https://suicidepreventionlifeline.org

(800) 273-8255

(888) 628-9454 (en Español)

(800) 799-4889 (for deaf and hard of hearing)

The National Suicide Prevention Lifeline is a national network of local crisis centers. It operates twenty-four hours a day and provides free and confidential support for people experiencing a suicidal crisis or emotional distress.

The Trevor Project

www.thetrevorproject.org

(866) 488-7386

The Trevor Project provides crisis intervention and suicide prevention services as well as a safe and judgment-free place to talk for LGBTQ individuals under age twenty-five. Its website provides information on sexual orientation and gender identity.

World Health Organization (WHO)
www.who.int
The WHO is the United Nations agency that promotes health worldwide. Its website contains the latest information about anxiety and depression from a global perspective.

Books

A.W. Buckey, *Teens and Depression*. San Diego, CA: Reference Point, 2021.

Tammy Gagne, *Teens and Anxiety*. San Diego, CA: ReferencePoint, 2021.

Celina McManus, *Understanding Anxiety*. San Diego, CA: ReferencePoint, 2020.

Katie Morton, *Are u ok? A Guide to Caring for Your Mental Health*. New York: Da Capo, 2018.

Sheri L. Turrell et al., *The Mindfulness and Acceptance Workbook for Teen Anxiety*. Oakland, CA: Instant Help, 2018.

Internet Sources

Centers for Disease Control and Prevention, "Anxiety and Depression in Children: Get the Facts," 2021. www.cdc.gov.

Jan Hoffman, "Young Adults Report Rising Levels of Anxiety and Depression in Pandemic," *New York Times*, August 13, 2020. www.nytimes.com.

Jacqueline Howard, "Suicide Attempts Rose Among Adolescent Girls During Pandemic, ER Data Suggest," CNN, June 11, 2011. www.cnn.com.

Phil Reed, "Anxiety and Social Media Use," *Digital World, Real World* (blog), *Psychology Today*, February 3, 2020. www.psychologytoday.com.